WITHDRAWN

THE SURPRISE PARTY

Adapted by **Chelsea Beyl**
Based on the episode written by **Jeff King**
Illustrated by **Imaginism Studio** and the **Disney Storybook Art Team**

ABDOBOOKS.COM

Reinforced library bound edition published in 2020 by Spotlight, a division of ABDO, PO Box 398166, Minneapolis, Minnesota 55439. Spotlight produces high-quality reinforced library bound editions for schools and libraries. Published by agreement with Disney Press, an imprint of Disney Book Group.

Printed in the United States of America, North Mankato, Minnesota.
092019   012020

DISNEP PRESS
New York • Los Angeles

THIS BOOK CONTAINS
RECYCLED MATERIALS

Library of Congress Control Number: 2019942031

Publisher's Cataloging-in-Publication Data

Names: Beyl, Chelsea; King, Jeff, authors. | Imaginism Studio; Disney Storybook Art Team, illustrators.
Title: Vampirina: the surprise party / by Chelsea Beyl and Jeff King; illustrated by Imaginism Studio and Disney Storybook Art Team.
Other title: the surprise party
Description: Minneapolis, Minnesota : Spotlight, 2020. | Series: World of reading level pre-1
Summary: Vee throws a spooky surprise party and is in for a surprise herself.
Identifiers: ISBN 9781532143953 (lib. bdg.)
Subjects: LCSH: Vampirina (Television program)--Juvenile fiction. | Vampires--Juvenile fiction. | Surprise parties--Juvenile fiction. | Friendship in children--Juvenile fiction. | Readers (Primary)--Juvenile fiction.
Classification: DDC [E]--dc23

Spotlight
A Division of ABDO
abdobooks.com

Vampirina is having a party.
It is a surprise. Demi invites
Vee's friends.

Poppy and Bridget cannot wait to surprise Vee.

"Can you come to my party?" Vee asks.
Does Vee know about the surprise?

"The surprise is not for me,"
says Vee.

"The surprises are for my friends."

Vee gets ready for the party.
Poppy hopes it is not too spooky.

Vee's friends show up.

"Boo!" Vee shouts. Her friends
are surprised!

"Boo!" says Vee's mom.

"AHHHH!" Vee's friends shout.

"Boo!" says Demi.
Vee's friends run.

"BOOO!"

Vee's friends see a mummy!
They are spooked!

Vee's friends run away.
"Come back!" shouts Vee.

Vee is sad.
Her friends did not like her party.

Edgar got a video of the
spooky surprises.
He thinks they were fake.
Poppy gets an idea.

Later, Poppy finds Vee.

"I liked your party!" Poppy says.
"And our friends like you."

Vee goes inside.
Her friends shout, "Surprise!"

There is one more surprise.
Vee's friends made a video.

Her friends say what
they love about Vee.
"I love her bat-tails," says Bridget.

"She shares her lunch," says a boy.

"Her house is spooky," says Edgar.
"That is cool!"

"We love you, Vee!" Poppy says.

Vee is surprised. Her friends love her even though she is not like them.

Vee's friends are
not spooked anymore.
Edgar told them the
spooky surprises were fake.

Time to party!